Mom Goes To W

Written by Libby Gleeson

Illustrated by Penny Azar

Scholastic Inc.
NEW YORK   TORONTO   LONDON   AUCKLAND   SYDNEY

It's early morning.

Everyone is arriving at school.

It's noisy and busy. Mai and Mark say
hello to everyone. Mom is going to work.

"Bye, Mom."
"Bye."

Nadia's mother is a student.
She goes to classes

and then reads
in the library.

She writes in a folder
and talks with the teacher
about her work.

Nadia paints a picture
for her mom.

Then she and Jack
build a city with blocks.

It takes a very long time.

Max's mother is a nurse.
She gives medicine
to her patients

and makes them comfortable.

She checks all the machines
and talks to the doctor
about each sick person.

Max plays in the dress-up corner.

He and Ann put the dolls to bed

and then join the others for music and a story.

Laurence's mother makes clothes in a factory.

She sews the clothes on her sewing machine

and sometimes she helps cut out the material.

Laurence and Georgia empty the ragbag on the floor.

They stick different-colored pieces on the big sheet of paper to hang on the wall.

At group time it's their turn to play on the big drum.

Rosie and Jack's mother works at home with their new baby. She feeds and bathes him.

While he's sleeping, she washes the clothes and cleans the house.

Later she takes him shopping in the carriage.

Rosie, Jack, and Nadia wash
all the dolls and teddy bears
and put them out to dry.

They empty the water onto
the dirt and make
a big mud pie.

Then it's time to
scrub their hands and
sit down to lunch.

After lunch, it's quiet time.

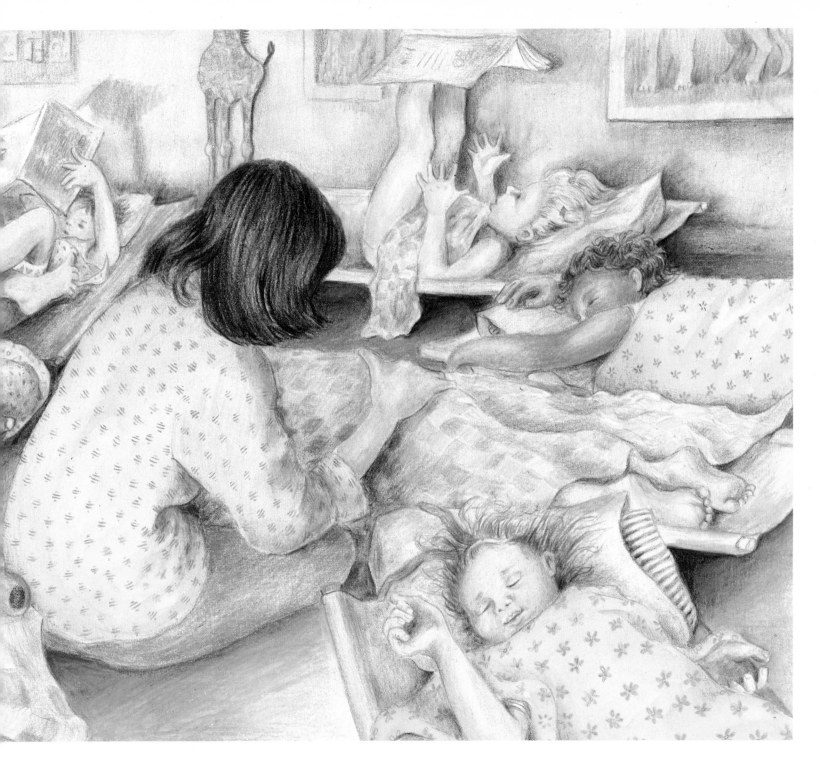

Mai pats Louis to sleep.

Georgia's and Louis's
mothers have government jobs.

Louis's mother is a secretary.
She opens the mail,
types the letters,
and answers the phone.

Georgia's mother is a
gardener. She mows the
lawns, digs, and plants
the tiny seedlings.

Georgia and Louis wake up
from their nap and
give Mark a hug.

They go outside to water
the vegetable patch
and pick some flowers.

They each make
long pasta necklaces
for their mothers.

Ann's mother is a potter.
She makes cups and bowls
on the wheel.

Then she adds the handles,
paints them,

and puts them in the
kiln for firing.

After her rest,
Ann puts away the cushions,

and then makes
fat farm animals
from play dough.

Later, she and Khen
run outside to swing
from the long rope that
hangs from the treehouse.

Brigit's mother works
in the supermarket.
She unpacks the boxes

and puts the tins and
packets on the shelves.

Sometimes she takes
the customers'
money at the checkout.

Brigit and Max play store.
They have lots of packets
and jars on the table

and a box of play money.

When they finish, they help
Mai cut up apples and
celery for an afternoon snack.

Khen's mother is a teacher.
She reads to her class

and helps the children
write their own stories.

After they go home, she
prepares work for the
next morning.

Khen and Ann help Mark
put the bikes away.

Then Khen takes all the
dolls and teddies
into the quiet corner

and shows them
some picture books.

It's almost time to go home.

Everyone is feeling tired.

"See you tomorrow."

"Bye."

For Pam, Bobby and all at
Sydney Lady Gowrie Child Centre,
with love and thanks.

ISBN 0-590-46288-1

Text copyright © 1992 by Libby Gleeson. Illustrations copyright © 1992
by Penny Azar. All rights reserved. Published by Scholastic Inc.,
555 Broadway, New York, NY 10012, by arrangement with Ashton
Scholastic.

The illustrations in this book were made with watercolor and
colored pencils.

12 11 10 9 8 7 6 5 4 3 2 1   5 6 7 8 9/9 0/0

Printed in U.S.A.   08

First Scholastic printing, December 1995